Here Comes
Doctor Hippo

Jonathan London

ILLUSTRATED BY Gilles Eduar

BOYDS MILLS PRESS

Honesdale, Pennsylvania

For Helene, Evelyn, and Claire, and for sweet Maureen
—JL

For Ricardo Ghelman
—GE

Text copyright © 2012 by Jonathan London
Illustrations copyright © 2012 by Gilles Eduar
All rights reserved
For information about permission to reproduce selections from
this book, please contact permissions@highlights.com.

Boyds Mills Press, Inc.
815 Church Street
Honesdale, Pennsylvania 18431

ISBN: 978-1-59078-851-6

Library of Congress Control Number: 2011940122

First edition
Printed in China
The text is set in Baileywick Gothic.
The illustrations are painted in gouache.
10 9 8 7 6 5 4 3 2 1

Little Hippo didn't like being little. In fact, he liked to dress up and pretend that he was big. So, one day he marched outside to play doctor.

When he came to Big Hippo, he said, "Hello! I am Doctor Hippo, and I am here to examine your big teeth! Please say *ahhh!*"

"Yuck!" cried Doctor Hippo. "Your breath smells like marsh muck!"
Big Hippo clapped his mouth shut, and Doctor Hippo went on his way.

Then he came to Very Tall Giraffe. He climbed a very tall ladder and said, "Hello! I am Doctor Hippo, and I am here to examine your tongue! Please stick it way out."

Giraffe opened his mouth . . . and licked Doctor Hippo with the longest and stickiest tongue in the world.

Sluuuuuurrrrrrrrrrrrrp!

"Eeeeewwwww!"
cried Doctor Hippo.
And he zipped off to find his next patient.

Now he came to Giant Crocodile. "Hello! I am Doctor Hippo,

and I am here to examine your—

SNAP!—
scaly skin!" cried Doctor Hippo, jumping away just in time.

Next he came to Laughing Hyena. "Hello!" he said.
"I am Doctor Hippo, and I am here to examine your calloused feet!
Please roll onto your back."

"That tickles!" laughed Hyena.

Hee-hee! Ha-ha! Ho-ho!

Hyena kicked his legs hard, and Doctor Hippo ran off, lickety-split.

Soon he found Elephant by the river.

"Hello! I am Doctor Hippo, and I am here to examine your big
ears and your long nose!" But when he looked in Elephant's very long nose,
Elephant sneezed . . . .

Aaaaaaa-CHOOOOOOO!

Doctor Hippo tumbled away . . .

and rolled right up to Lion's feet.
"Um . . . I am Doctor Hippo, and I am here to examine your eyes."
They were big and squinty and very scary.

RAAAAAAHHHRRRRRRR!

roared Lion.

"YIIIIIIKES!" cried Doctor Hippo. And he ran, wailing . . .

. . . all the way home.
"What's the matter, Little Hippo?" cried Mama Hippo.
"I've been playing doctor," he said, hiccuping and wiping his eyes.

"I saw Big Hippo, Very Tall Giraffe, Giant Crocodile, Laughing Hyena, Elephant, and Lion! But Lion roared at me and now I don't feel so well."

"Oh dear!" said Mama Hippo.
"Let's see what I can do. Say *ahhh!*"
"*Aaaaaaahhhhh!*" said Little Hippo.
"Your teeth are big and white," said Mama Hippo.
"And your breath smells like . . . peppermint!"
Little Hippo stopped sniffling.

"Now stick out your tongue," said Mama Hippo.
Little Hippo stuck it *waaaay* out.
"Your tongue is as pink as a rose petal," she said.
"And your skin is as soft as a peach!"

Mama Hippo helped put on Little Hippo's pajamas
with a SNAP! and said, "Now let me examine your feet."

Little Hippo rolled onto his back . . . and started giggling.
"That tickles!" he cried.

HEE-HEE! HA-HA! HO-HO!

Now Mama Hippo tickled his nose . . .
and Little Hippo sneezed.
Aaaaaaa-CHOOOO!
" 'Scuse me!" He grinned from ear to ear.

Mama Hippo looked into his clear, bright eyes and said, "You're a very healthy hippo!"

Then she gave him a huge hug . . . and put him to bed.
"Sleep tight, Doctor Hippo!"
"Good night, Doctor Mommy!"